A Home for
POPPY PLATYPUS

Written by **Kristen Brown**
Illustrated by **Marta Maszkiewicz**

A Home for
POPPY PLATYPUS

To Joey for being a constant through every twist and turn.

To Kennedy for teaching me what it means to be a mom.

To Caroline for being the missing piece I can't imagine living without.

And to every child who has ever been fostered or adopted—

you are special...you are cherished...you are loved.

One crisp, cool morning the Beaver family of three bundled up and ventured out of their lodge to take a stroll around the pond. Winter had ended, and all around the poppies were beginning to bloom, announcing the arrival of spring.

Mommy Beaver, Daddy Beaver and little Bella Beaver had just arrived at the pond when they found, nestled in some soft, green grass, an egg. "Now, who could this egg belong to?" wondered Mommy Beaver. The three beavers looked around and saw no one nearby.

A cool wind blew and the three beavers shivered. Mommy Beaver was worried about the egg getting cold without a mother to keep it warm, so she took off her scarf and gently tucked it around the egg. "Daddy, why don't you and Bella go see if you can find out who this egg belongs to? I will stay here and keep it warm," she suggested. So off they went.

They had just gotten to the other side of the pond when they found a pair of ducks. "Good morning, Ms. Duck!" called Daddy Beaver. "Are you missing an egg?"

"Why certainly not," replied Ms. Duck. "All of our eggs have already hatched." And she stood up to reveal four fluffy, yellow ducklings huddled together beneath her. "Congratulations!" yelled Daddy Beaver as he and little Bella continued on.

Next, they met a Mother Deer and her young fawn walking out from the woods. "Daddy, let's ask them," whispered little Bella. "But honey, deer don't lay eggs," Daddy replied. "Can we please just ask?" pleaded little Bella, who was growing more concerned about finding the egg's mother. Daddy Beaver nodded. "Hello, Ms. Deer," said little Bella. "We found an egg and are looking for its mother. Have you lost one?"

"Not us," replied Ms. Deer, "we are on our morning walk to the pond. I do hope you find who you are looking for though." "Thank you," said little Bella and they continued on.

Daddy Beaver and little Bella Beaver came to a small, dark cave and found a Mother Bear and her two young cubs taking their first steps out into the bright sunlight. "Good morning," said Daddy Beaver, "are you missing an egg?" "Surely not. My cubs and I just finished hibernating and are hoping to find some fresh berries for breakfast," said Ms. Bear as she and her cubs began slowly walking away. So, Daddy Beaver and Bella Beaver continued on.

Not long after, Bella heard a loud, fast tapping noise coming from up above and saw a Mother Woodpecker and her three chicks. "Good morning, Ms. Woodpecker!" shouted Bella way up into the treetop. "Are you missing an egg?" "No, sorry, dearie!" replied Ms. Woodpecker, as she and her chicks quickly went back to hammering into the tree in search of bugs. Beginning to feel discouraged, Daddy Beaver and Bella Beaver continued on.

A short time later Bella heard a scurrying near her feet and looked down to see a Mother Chipmunk with her four pups. Little Bella bent down. "Hello, Ms. Chipmunk," she said, "We found a lost egg. Are you missing one?" "All of my little ones are here," answered Ms. Chipmunk. "We are hoping to find some delicious nuts," added the smallest pup. "We ate all of ours this winter." "Thanks anyway," sighed little Bella as she and Daddy Beaver continued on.

Feeling quite discouraged they had not yet found the missing egg's family, Daddy Beaver and little Bella Beaver started back towards the pond. As they walked little Bella felt troubled. Surely the egg had a mother, so where was she? What was going to happen to the little egg without a mother to care for it?

They found Mommy Beaver sitting quietly, humming a soft lullaby and rocking gently back and forth. "We asked everyone we could find, but no one was missing an egg," said Daddy Beaver. "The egg is not a duck, it's not a deer, it's not a bear, it's not a woodpecker, and it's not a chipmunk."

"That's okay, I think I may have found her family after all," whispered Mommy Beaver, as she gently uncovered a tiny baby platypus, sound asleep, snuggled up in her arms. "What do you think Bella? Is there room in the family for one more?" Little Bella stopped to think for a moment. "Well, I have always wanted a sister," she replied "and I know just the name." And she looked around at all of the beautiful poppies.

And so, the family of four set off together,
excited to bring baby Poppy home.

2